My Journey

A Christmas Tail

With many Christmas blessings!

Kevin & Anne MacMillan

Kevin and Anne MacMillan

MATZO'S JOURNEY
Copyright © 2018 by Kevin and Anne MacMillan

Scripture quotations marked NIV are taken from the Holy Bible, NEW INTERNATIONAL VERSION®. Copyright © 1973, 1978, 1984, 2011 by Biblica, Inc. All rights reserved worldwide. Used by permission. NEW INTERNATIONAL VERSION® and NIV® are registered trademarks of Biblica, Inc. Use of either trademark for the offering of goods or services requires the prior written consent of Biblica US, Inc. Scripture quotations marked NKJV are taken from the New King James Version®. Copyright © 1982 by Thomas Nelson, Inc. Used by permission. All rights reserved. Scripture quotations marked CEV are taken from the Contemporary English Version © 1991, 1992, 1995 by American Bible Society, Used by Permission. Scripture quotations marked NLT are taken from the Holy Bible, New Living Translation, copyright ©1996, 2004, 2007 by Tyndale House Foundation. Used by permission of Tyndale House Publishers, Inc., Carol Stream, Illinois 60188. All rights reserved. Scripture quotations marked ESV are taken from the Holy Bible, English Standard Version. ESV® Permanent Text Edition® (2016). Copyright © 2001 by Crossway Bibles, a publishing ministry of Good News Publishers.

Printed in Canada

ISBN: 978-1-4866-1516-2

Word Alive Press
119 De Baets Street, Winnipeg, MB R2J 3R9
www.wordalivepress.ca

Cataloguing in Publication may be obtained through Library and Archives Canada

Matzo's Journey is lovingly dedicated to our grandchildren, Avery, Ashley, Luke, Emery, Heidi and Sidney.

But from everlasting to everlasting the LORD's love is with those who fear him, and his righteousness with their children's children.

—Psalm 103:17, NIV

Contents

Introduction

Welcome to *Matzo's Journey,* the first book in a trilogy that is intended to be read aloud daily through the month of December in the place of an Advent calendar. It's not only about the Saviour's birth; it's also a story of learning to trust God. When Mary and her pet mouse, Matzo, hear the angel Gabriel announce that she will give birth to the Saviour, they receive the news joyfully. Joseph and his turtledove, Tabitha, need a visit from the angel before they can truly believe. And yet, throughout the story all of them will face their own doubts and fears as Joseph builds the family home, Mary and Matzo leave for Jerusalem to visit Elizabeth and Zacharias, and Joseph, Mary and the animals make the long trip from Nazareth to Bethlehem with its adventures and dangers.

Throughout the story they learn that God and His Word can be trusted. Even when things look difficult—when they feel there is no way out of their predicaments—they remember the words of the angel reassuring them of God's faithfulness and His power to bring His promises to pass.

As we read the story that culminates in the birth of Jesus, let us also remember that "nothing is impossible for God."

chapter one

Sudden Courage

"What is *that?*" It looked like a fire was blazing in Mary's room! But there was no smoke, and the rest of the house looked normal. Matzo couldn't understand it, but he was already scurrying toward the house to protect her. "Mary needs my help," he said to himself with a quivering voice. "She's my dearest friend, and I can't let her down now!"

Then he saw something that made him stop in his tracks—Festus! Festus was a nasty stray cat who lived nearby, and there he was with his buddy Horatio. The two of them were out looking for food, as usual. Matzo didn't know what to do. If they caught him, he was in big trouble. Matzo, you see, was a mouse. And cats love to chase mice—and worse, they love to eat them!

Matzo thought that he wouldn't be able to get to the house, but then he looked up again and saw the fiery glow from Mary's room. He had to get there somehow, but Festus and Horatio would notice him if he tried to sneak by them.

Right in between the two prowling cats was a big old log. Matzo said to himself, "If I can't get by them without being seen, maybe I can at least slow them down." When their backs were turned to him, he scooted over to the log and jumped on top of it. Surprising himself with his own courage, he shouted, "Hi, boys! How's the hunting goin'?"

The two hungry cats turned and saw little Matzo staring at them. Matzo looked back and forth at one, then the other, but didn't move. The log was so big that the two cats couldn't see each other over it, and Matzo knew that.

Festus and Horatio couldn't believe their eyes. Here, right in front of them, was the little mouse they'd been chasing all year! And he was too close to get away. They both crouched down, waiting for just the right time to pounce.

Then they jumped, heading straight for poor little Matzo. But just as they were about to land right on him, he jumped up as high as he could. Their heads clunked into each other, and they both fell down, dizzy.

Matzo rushed toward the house. There was a tiny crack at the bottom of the front door where he had squeezed through many times before. But he had to hurry. Festus and Horatio had picked themselves up and caught his scent, and they were getting closer, and closer, and closer!

When Matzo was almost at the door, they were so close he could feel their smelly breath down his little neck! Suddenly he heard a booming voice. "You cats get out of here!" It was Heli, Mary's father. He smacked them with the broom that he was using to sweep the front step. Heli had never liked cats, especially Festus and Horatio, so he was pleased give them a good scare. "And never come back," he yelled as they ran away. But Heli

missed a wee little mouse pushing his way through the small opening in his own front door.

Matzo headed straight for Mary's room. Everyone else was outside helping Heli with the evening chores, so it was safe for him to dash right across the living room floor.

As he got closer to Mary's room, he could see the bright light shimmering from underneath her door. He wanted to protect her, but something about the light made Matzo feel that Mary was actually safe. And when he made his way through the small crack under the door, he looked in amazement. He couldn't believe his eyes! It wasn't a fire! It was...

To be continued tomorrow...

chapter two

An Unexpected Visitor

Matzo was speechless—he had never seen anything like it, or rather, any*one* like it. He forgot all about the cats, the log, and Heli's broom. Matzo was looking at…an angel. And what a sight! The angel shimmered with light that changed from one colour to another and always moved, flickering like flames. He had huge, beautiful wings on his back and was clothed in—well, in light! He was as tall as the ceiling, and yet he was kneeling before Mary.

Matzo realized that the angel was *talking* with her. He had the richest, fullest and most soothing voice he had ever heard. Matzo wasn't afraid, and yet he was. He saw that Mary wasn't afraid, and yet she was. She rubbed her thumb against her first finger, and she only did that when she was nervous.

The angel said, "His name will be Jesus. He will be great and will be called the Son of the Most High."[1]

Jesus—a beautiful name that means "salvation." Matzo wondered who this Jesus was and what he would save them from.

Now Mary was speaking to the glorious being who knelt in front of her. "How can this happen? I'm not yet married. A girl can't have a child if she's not married."

Matzo thought, *A child? Who's having a child?*

The angel replied to Mary, "The Holy Spirit will come down to you, and God's power will come over you. So your child will be called the holy Son of God."[2]

Matzo couldn't believe his ears—Mary was going to have a child? But she was young, and his best friend at that! Mary meant a lot to him. She also meant a lot to Joseph. In fact, they were planning to get married soon (and Matzo was trying to figure out a way to move with Mary after the wedding). But he knew beyond a shadow of a doubt that what the angel said was all true.

Suddenly, he realized he hadn't been listening. The angel was speaking again in that smooth, powerful voice. "No one thought she could ever have a baby, but in three months she will have a son."[3]

Now Matzo was really confused. *It sounds like someone else is going to have a baby—I wonder who.*

But the last words the angel spoke rang in Matzo's ears: "Nothing is impossible for God!"[4]

Mary's face was shining in the gleaming light of her angelic visitor. She said, "I am the Lord's servant! Let it happen as you have said."[5]

And then, knowing his task was finished, the angel vanished.

Mary stood silently for a while, and so did little Matzo. Soon he tiptoed over closer to her, and she looked down, surprised.

"Matzo!" she said softly, with a quiver in her voice. "Did you see the beautiful angel?" She could see by the expression on his face that he indeed had. "Oh, Matzo, I don't exactly know what to do. Everything has changed! He told me I am going to have a baby—*the Son of God!*" She put her hands on her tummy, looked up and said, "Heavenly Father, give me strength for this journey!"

Matzo didn't know everything, but he knew it was time to be quiet.

They both knelt and prayed.

To be continued tomorrow...

chapter three

Finding Tabitha

As quiet as a mouse, Matzo slipped out of Mary's room while she continued to pray. He couldn't help her right then, and he needed to get some rest after such an exciting day. So he found a comfy spot and fell fast asleep.

First thing in the morning, he went to find Tabitha to tell her the news. Tabitha was a turtledove who belonged to Joseph, Mary's fiancé, and she and Matzo had become friends as Joseph and Mary got to know one another. He wanted to tell her what was going on because it was so very important. When was the last time *you* had an angel come to you and make such an important announcement?

As he scurried along the pathway to Joseph's house, Matzo thought about his dearest friend, Mary. Life was going to change for her, and he wasn't sure how it would all turn out for him. With a baby coming, she wouldn't have as much time for Matzo as she used to.

Matzo loved Mary dearly, and she loved him as well. He had grown up in her home, although Heli would have preferred that he live outside. But many times Mary said to her father, "Oh, Abba, he's such a cute little mouse! Please let him stay with us." Heli couldn't say no to such a request. Little Matzo made Mary happy, and like any father he loved to see his daughter happy. Life was not always easy living in Nazareth with King Herod and the Romans in control. You never quite knew what the nasty soldiers were going to do, so what harm could it cause to have a little mouse in their home?

As Mary did her daily chores, she and Matzo played together. He thought he was helping her keep the floor clean by eating up all the crumbs that fell from the table. But really, mice aren't very good at keeping things tidy. And Mary was happy to clean up after him.

She also sang lovely Hebrew songs that helped him forget about Festus and Horatio. She had a beautiful and melodious voice, while Matzo's sounded high and squeaky. Maybe that's why Joseph called him Pipsqueak rather than Matzo. It wasn't his favourite nickname, but he put up with it because Mary loved Joseph so much.

Matzo got to Joseph's house without even a sign of the two stray cats who were after him the night before. Perhaps Heli's broom was still fresh in their minds. As he got near, he could see Tabitha circling overhead. Her broken wing seemed to be much better. "Hello, Matzo!" she sang as she flew lower and lower. "It's such a beautiful day—hardly a cloud in the sky!"

"We don't have time for that!" cried Matzo. "I've got some amazing news!"

Tabitha was surprised—she had never seen Matzo so excited before. "What's so amazing? Did Festus and Horatio let you keep your tail this morning? Did Mary forget to feed you, so you're here looking for some breakfast? Or does King Herod need a new mouse in his palace?"

"Oh, Tabitha, stop being so silly! I've seen something *really* amazing! Mary was visited by an *angel* last night, and he said she's going to have a baby, and that baby is going to be a Saviour, the Son of God!"

"A baby? A Saviour? The Son of God? Come on, Matzo—you've been eating too much peanut butter. Joseph said just the other day that we haven't had a prophetic voice for 400 years. Do you suppose God is going to use a mouse to be the prophet of Israel?"

Matzo said, "Well, why not? Nothing is impossible for God!" He paused for a second. "And what's a prophet?"

"A prophet is a person who speaks for God, like Isaiah or Jeremiah. You know, they wrote things like 'Behold, the virgin shall conceive and bear a Son, and shall call His name Immanuel,'[6] not the stuff you're talking about."

After thinking for a minute, Matzo said, "But wait a minute. This isn't about me—it's about Mary. It's about the angel. It's about the Son of God...and that last thing you said sounds just like what I'm talking about!"

"I think Festus clobbered you on the head once too often. I'd never believe something like that unless I saw the angel *myself*," said Tabitha.

"Well," said Matzo, "like I said, nothing is impossible for God!"

To be continued tomorrow...

chapter four

A Bit About Joseph

"Whatever happens, life is going to be different for Mary and me. And it's going to be different for Joseph too. Hey, that reminds me, is Joseph working on the new house?" asked Matzo.

Tabitha said, "Yes, he started soon after sunrise this morning. Do you want to go have a look?"

"Yes, let's see how he's doing."

As they made their way over to where Joseph was working, the sound of a pounding hammer and the smell of fresh sawdust greeted them. Tabitha said, "I've never seen anyone work as hard as Joseph. He's been at it every day for the last three weeks! Well, not on the Sabbath, of course." You see, the Sabbath is a day once a week when the Jewish people stop working so they can rest. God created the heavens and the earth in six days and then rested on the seventh. He told man to do the same—to work for six days and then rest. But the Sabbath had been the day before, so Joseph was at it again.

Not only was he a hard worker, but he was very good at what he did. He was a carpenter, so house-building came naturally to him. When he was young, his father taught him how to use carpenters' tools, and he had learned well. Joseph had also learned how to lay stone. While he wasn't the fastest worker, he was better than almost anyone else, even his father.

"He's taking a little longer than most carpenters would," said Tabitha, "but it will be the best house in Nazareth! One thing that slows him down is that he keeps helping other people. His work is well-known, and so many people want to hire him."

"Hmm," said Matzo, "and he finds it hard to say no, doesn't he?"

"You're right—he's so kind, and he doesn't like to disappoint people, so he sometimes takes on more work than he should. And he always works until a job is done. He just won't be rushed. There is nothing half-hearted about him!"

Tabitha continued, "In fact, I heard that several years ago his aunt Rebekah thought he should marry the rabbi's daughter! She said he was getting on in years and needed a wife. But he knew she wasn't the right one, and he was willing to wait. He was patient, and he was rewarded with Mary."

"He's a patient man, but all the same, I hope he gets the house finished in time," said Matzo.

"Oh, don't worry; he will!"

The house was starting to come together. Lots of work still needed to be done, but you could see that it was going to be beautiful. Not every young bride was treated to such a special home, but then Mary was a very special girl.

Matzo hoped that Joseph would let a pet mouse live in the new house. Surely Joseph would want Mary to have help keeping the house clean (especially with a new baby), so surely there would be a place for him! He could help keep the crumbs cleaned up and would be good company for Tabitha.

Sawdust was abundant around Joseph's shop, just the kind mice like to use to make nests. Maybe Matzo would settle down with a wife one day too.

To be continued tomorrow...

chapter five

Mary Tells Her Parents

eli's house was quiet for the rest of the week. Mary kept to herself and did her work in silence. She seemed to be thinking a lot, and she knelt beside her bed when her chores were finished. Her parents and her brothers and sisters noticed the change in her. Normally Mary was cheerful and made everyone laugh. She teased her younger brothers and got after the little girls to work hard so that one day they would be good wives to someone as good and dear as Joseph and Abba. She always sang and asked questions, but this week she was quiet, and her parents wondered what was wrong.

One evening Matzo heard Festus and Horatio meowing outside the door. He was very glad to be in the house and hid himself in a corner of Mary's room. He heard footsteps coming toward her door and then a gentle knock.

Abba and Momma came inside the bedroom. "Mary, dear, you don't seem to be yourself this week. Are you feeling well? Did you and Joseph have a spat? Are you thinking that he's taking too long getting the house ready for you?" asked Momma.

"Oh, Abba, Momma, I've wanted to talk to you all week. My tongue has seemed to be in knots. Every evening I've walked toward your room when the children were in bed and then turned back," said Mary with tears in the corners of her large brown eyes. "I know that what I'm about to tell you will sound like a wild story, but please remember everything you've taught me since I was a child."

"You're talking in riddles, Mary," said Heli.

"Please tell us what has happened," said Momma.

"After the Sabbath was over and you and the children were doing evening chores, I was in my room preparing for the week to come," explained Mary. "All at once my room was filled with the most brilliant light you can imagine. It was as if the sun appeared before me."

"Mary, let me feel your head," said Momma. "Do you have a fever?"

"No, Momma. Please let me keep talking."

Matzo was standing on his hind legs with his eyes wide open, hoping to tell them, "Please listen to her. Please believe her—I saw the angel myself. She's telling the truth!"

"An angel appeared to me. He called himself Gabriel and told me that I am highly favoured by God. He said that of all women I am most blessed."

Momma gasped, and Abba's eyebrows lowered.

"He said I shouldn't be afraid, but God has chosen me—me, your little Mimi—to have a Son. I told him it was impossible, because I'm not married yet. He said that the Spirit of God will come upon me, and the Child will be the Son of the Most

17

High God and will have a Kingdom that will last forever and ever! He said that I'm to name Him Jesus."

Mary fell into her parents' arms and began to weep. "Abba, my whole life you've taught me that a Saviour will come to redeem us. Every day you've told us that Messiah will come. You've had us memorize the words of the prophets. Momma, Abba, the angel said that I will give birth to the Son of God."

Abba and Momma were stunned. Their eyes were like big saucers, and their mouths dropped open.

"Then the angel said that my cousin Elizabeth is also to have a son, in her old age," Mary said.

"You know this news?" asked Heli in wonder. "We just got word about it and haven't spoken of it to anyone. But you say the *angel* told you?"

"Yes, Abba! And he said, 'Nothing is impossible for God.' And then I said I am the Lord's servant—just like you've always told us—and I said let it be just as the angel said."

Heli asked, "Has Joseph been here this week, Mary?"

"No, Abba, you know he hasn't been here. How will I tell him this news? Can you please help me, Abba and Momma?"

Matzo felt he had to do something, so he headed out the door. Mary and her parents were hugging each other, praying and crying together. They weren't sad, but they needed to hug and cry because God had called their family to such a huge job. Over and over they repeated, "Nothing is impossible for God. Nothing is impossible for God."

To be continued tomorrow…

chapter six

A Nighttime Adventure

The door was locked, but Matzo knew a way out. He hadn't been eating as much this week with Mary acting differently. He was used to her passing him lots of goodies from the table, but this week he'd only eaten the crumbs that fell. That was okay; he was more concerned for Mary than for his little belly. And that would make it easier to slip under the door and scoot out into the night.

But there was that sound again…the low, hungry meows of the neighbourhood cats, Festus and Horatio. Matzo had to be careful. His ears were pretty sharp at picking up noises, and he could see well in the dark. He had a mission to accomplish, so he couldn't let a little fear stop him from outsmarting his adversaries (that's a big word for "enemies").

At the front door he saw a dirty sock that Mary's brother Ben had left lying on the floor. He decided to get inside it. This made it a little harder to get under the door, but with some squeezing and squishing he finally slipped through. The wind was blowing so he decided to pretend he was a dustball, and he rolled right past hungry Festus and angry Horatio! Thanks to Ben's smelly feet, the cats didn't pick up on Matzo's scent; they just covered their noses, and away he rolled until he was out of their sight!

When he got to the road, Matzo left the sock in the ditch so he could use it again when he needed it. He was sure no one would take it. Who likes dirty, smelly socks anyway?

He had a mission, and that was to get to Tabitha and tell her about Mary and her parents. Mary needed help telling Joseph her news, and Matzo wanted to lend a hand, or in his case a paw.

Bright stars and planets shone in the sky and gave Matzo a little light as he made his way to Joseph's house.

When he arrived he heard a pleasant cooing sound from his friend Tabitha, who was fast asleep in Joseph's open window. He made some subtle squeaks and "pssst" sounds and a few mousy coughs, but all he heard in return was a big snort as Tabitha rolled over in her nest and began snoring.

Matzo laughed and laughed and laughed. He had never heard anything as funny as Tabitha's snoring, and after all the nervousness around his house, he just needed a good belly laugh.

At that moment Tabitha woke up. "Who's down there?" she called out. "Stop, thief! What scallywag is trying to disturb Joseph of Nazareth from his God-given rest?"

"Relax, Tabitha. Relax," called out Matzo. He thought it was pretty fun to have awakened her this way. "It's me, Matzo. We have to talk."

"How do I know it's you? I can't see you! What if you're an enemy soldier with Caesar's guard?"

Matzo laughed even harder. The thought of him being a soldier was too ridiculous! He was a mouse, not a man, even though he seemed to be getting braver by the day.

"Come on, Tabitha, wake up! We have to talk. There's important stuff happening, and Joseph and Mary need us!"

"Okay, okay. Now I believe it's you, Matzo. Why don't you crawl up the stone wall and sit up in this windowsill with me. That way I can stay warm and we can see each other," said Tabitha.

Matzo was pretty good at climbing up walls, but it took him three tries before he made it up to where Tabitha was perched. This time she was the one laughing. It was pretty funny to see the little mouse climbing up Joseph's neatly laid stones and sliding back down, landing right on his backside!

"Wow," said Matzo, "that's the first time all week I've had a good laugh."

"Me too," replied Tabitha. "I still don't believe your 'mouse tales' of angels and babies, but I've felt tense since you were here earlier this week. So why are you here in the middle of the night?"

"We need to get Joseph over to Heli's house in the morning," said Matzo with the strongest voice he could muster.

"In the morning? That will take a miracle!" replied Tabitha. "Joseph works from dawn to dusk. He's got more to do than he has time to do it. He'll never leave his shop to go visiting during the day."

"Well," said Matzo, "that's why I'm here talking to you now. We have to make a plan!"

To be continued tomorrow...

chapter seven

News for Joseph

As soon as daylight peeked over the horizon, Matzo and Tabitha began to put their plan to work. Joseph had been up for an hour—praying, reciting the Torah and getting ready for the day. He was just wiping the crumbs from breakfast off his face when Matzo slipped under the door and squeaked as loudly as he could.

You see, the animals could talk to each other, but the people couldn't understand them, so Matzo and Tabitha needed to get Joseph's attention like regular animals do today. Dogs bark, cats meow, and mice squeak!

Joseph stuck his finger in his ear and rubbed hard. Then the squeaking got louder and longer. His eyes looked to the spot where the noise came from, and to his surprise, there was Matzo.

"Pipsqueak, what are you doing here at this time of the morning?" asked Joseph with a smile on his face. "Are things okay at Heli's house? How's Mary?" As he asked, he opened the door to see if Matzo had come by himself.

Tabitha flew inside and began to fly in circles around Matzo. They had worked this out ahead of time. They really wanted to get Joseph's attention, and it was working!

Joseph put his sandals on, grabbed a coat and said, "Come on, friends. I don't know why you are acting this way, but it makes me think that I need to get over to Heli's house and check on them. Is Mary okay, Matzo?"

The very fact that Joseph didn't call Matzo by his nickname was evidence that he was in no mood for joking around and wanted to find out what was causing the animals to act so strangely.

The road was empty except for one old beggar, who was heading in the opposite direction. Joseph called to him, "If you need a meal later on, stop by the workshop, and I'll share something with you. Right now, I have no time to talk and help." The beggar nodded and gave a toothless smile to Joseph and Matzo while he waved to Tabitha, who flew overhead.

Joseph was running, and Matzo found it very hard to keep up. His little paws were barely touching the ground as he followed Joseph back to Mary's house. Tabitha flew ahead and cooed softly as she landed in Mary's windowsill.

This brought Mary to the window. She looked outside and saw Joseph running toward the house. She blushed, and then her eyes filled up with tears. She hadn't expected to see Joseph today, but it seemed her prayers were answered, and she would be able to tell him the news about the baby, the angel and the plan God had revealed.

She ran to the kitchen, where her Momma was tidying up the breakfast dishes. "Momma, Momma, I see Joseph coming down the lane. He's running. Do you think an angel has spoken to him, Momma?"

Momma took a deep breath and called, "Heli, Heli, please come to the front door. We have a visitor!"

Heli was in the back room reciting some psalms. He called back, "And who comes calling before the sun has fully risen in the sky?" Then he said to himself, "Are we to entertain angels in this humble home again this morning?"

At that moment a knock sounded at the door. Heli opened it slowly, surprised to see Joseph on the other side. "Joseph, Joseph, my boy. What brings you here so early on a workday? Is the house finished? Are you coming to claim your bride? You have been running as quickly as Elijah's whirlwind!"

"Heli, Deborah, Mary—" he stuttered. "I'm, I'm here… I'm here because the mouse Matzo and my bird, Tabitha, were acting so strangely, and I thought something must be wrong. *Is* there anything wrong?"

"Have a seat, Joseph. We wanted to see you soon. I think that the Lord brought you here this morning. Can you imagine that He used a bird and a mouse? Ah, nothing is impossible for God," Heli whispered.

Momma asked, "Joseph, can I make you some tea? You must need something to drink; you've been running."

"I don't need tea. I just need to know what's happening. Why did I need to come here so early this morning?"

So for the next hour Heli, Mary, Momma and Joseph sat together. It was very quiet, and Tabitha couldn't hear anything from the window. Matzo was so hungry that he stopped by the chicken coop to eat some grain. When he peeked under the crack in the front door he could see the side of Joseph's face, and the muscles around his jaw were tightening. He was holding his head in his hands and staring at the floor.

"I have to think...I have to pray. And Mrs. Cohen needs her rocking chair built. I'm going back to work. I don't know what to think about what you've told me." Joseph headed toward the door. "I will come by in a few days." He looked at Mary and her parents with heavy eyes and said, "Goodbye, Mary. Goodbye, Heli. I need to go."

Joseph stepped on Matzo's tail as he left the house but didn't even notice. Tabitha could see that he wasn't sure about the story of the angel and the baby.

She watched Joseph plod down the lane and then flew over to the door where Matzo was holding his squashed tail. "What did I tell you, Matzo? I won't believe this story about an angel and a baby unless I see an angel myself—and it doesn't look like Joseph will either!"

She flapped her wings and flew after Joseph, who was walking slowly toward their house. He seemed lost in thought, so she flew on ahead without looking back at Matzo.

To be continued tomorrow...

chapter eight

Joseph's Special Visitor

Joseph walked home looking straight ahead of him. If you had seen him, you would have thought he knew exactly what he was doing. But he was confused—more confused than he had ever been in his life. He had been so sure about his future, his work...and his wife. But it all changed this morning. What was he supposed to think about the words Mary and her parents had told him? She was having a child—the Son of God—the Messiah?

Joseph had always believed that the Messiah was coming. His parents and the rabbis had taught him that. But the Messiah was going to be a king, and kings aren't born to poor village girls. It couldn't be—it didn't make sense! And yet, when he looked into Mary's eyes, and Heli's and Deborah's, he saw a peace and joy he could not explain.

"Can it be true?" he asked himself. "No—it's ridiculous! God wouldn't do something like that! He couldn't!" But he remembered what Heli had said: "Nothing is impossible for God."

Tabitha had flown ahead of him, and she was waiting for his arrival, perched in her favourite spot in his bedroom windowsill. She heard him repeating, "Nothing is impossible for God. Nothing is impossible for God." She thought, *Oh no, don't tell me he's starting to believe this! I wouldn't believe it unless I saw an angel myself!"*

Joseph walked into his room and carefully pulled out his Torah scroll. It was very precious to him, so he was very delicate with it. He said, "I am reminded of a verse in Jeremiah, but I can't remember where it is exactly." He looked and looked through the book, then stopped at one passage. "There is nothing too hard for You."[7] He stood up and repeated, "There *is* nothing too hard for You!" He closed his eyes and reached his hands up to heaven and said, "Oh God, please help me understand—please show me Your will so I can know what to do!"

He stood silently for a long time.

He had trusted God his whole life, and he knew that somehow God was going to answer his prayer.

After a while, he went into his workshop to finish Mrs. Cohen's rocking chair. He worked for a few minutes, but he couldn't concentrate. All he could think about was Mary and what she had told him. A strange tiredness came over him, so he went into his room and lay down.

Tabitha settled again on his windowsill so she could be close by. It was very unusual for him to lie down in the middle of the morning.

Joseph fell asleep quickly, and Tabitha decided to take a nap as well. But soon after she closed her eyes, she was aware of a brilliant light. She thought maybe the sun was in her eyes, so she opened them. The most beautiful creature she had ever seen was kneeling by Joseph's bed! He looked like a man but was much bigger, and he had wings like hers but far more beautiful and powerful. And he shone like the sun. It was hard to keep looking, but she couldn't take her eyes off him. She was looking at an angel!

Then he spoke. His voice was rich and powerful and yet gentle. "Joseph, the baby that Mary will have is from the Holy Spirit. Go ahead and marry her. Then after the baby is born, name him Jesus, because he will save his people from their sins."[8]

Then he faded from her view, and the room was normal again. Tabitha wanted to fly over and wake Joseph up, but she knew she shouldn't move. Something very special had just happened, and she didn't want to disturb anything.

Soon Joseph woke up from his dream, looking around with wide eyes. Then he dropped his head and said, "Thank You, Lord, for answering my prayer!" He lifted his eyes and said, "There is one more thing…"

Joseph opened his Torah scroll again, this time to the book of Isaiah. After searching, he read aloud, "'Behold, the virgin shall conceive and bear a Son, and shall call His name Immanuel.'[9] *Immanuel* means 'God with us.'" He paused. "The Son of God is 'God with us.' Oh, my Lord, I believe, I believe! Nothing is impossible for God!"

To be continued tomorrow…

chapter nine

Joseph Agrees

Joseph looked at Tabitha. "Tabitha, this is very special! This is very uncommon!" His bird was cooing with an unusual expression on her face. He didn't know that she was saying, "I know, Joseph! We have seen an angel from God Most High!"

"I must go talk to Mary. I told her I would be back in a few days, but God has changed everything!"

Tabitha cooed her approval as Joseph started walking down the path. Tabitha, meanwhile, flew on as fast as she could to Heli's house. She too had some news she needed to share with her friend Matzo.

Since she could fly so fast, she arrived well before Joseph, and she found Matzo just outside the front door, looking for some stray seeds or grain to eat.

"Matzo!" she exclaimed. "You'll never believe what happened! *I saw an angel!* He was the most beautiful thing I have ever seen. He was bigger than a man and had beautiful wings, and he came to visit Joseph!"

"That's wonderful!" said Matzo. "I wonder if it was the same angel I saw."

"No, no. You don't understand—I saw a *real* angel. He was shining like the sun, and the whole room was filled with light!"

Matzo said, "Yes, Tabitha, that's what I was trying to tell you."

"Oh Matzo," said Tabitha, "you still don't get it. I don't know what *you* saw, but it was nothing like this. His voice was powerful but soothing, and he delivered a message from God to Joseph."

Matzo had taken all he could take. He yelled at Tabitha (as loudly as a mouse can yell), "No, Tabitha—*you* don't understand! I saw a real angel too, and he came to deliver a message from God to Mary! We saw the same thing!"

Finally Tabitha understood that when Matzo came to tell her about seeing an angel, he was serious. They both witnessed something very, very special. God had an extraordinary plan for Joseph and Mary, and they got to be part of it!

"Get out of here!" yelled Joseph. Matzo dashed for the crack under the front door just as Festus landed right where he had been sitting. And Tabitha shot up in the air just out of the reach of Horatio's outstretched claws. Joseph had arrived just in time to save them from the two hungry cats, who had snuck up on them. That was a close call!

Joseph shooed the cats away, took a deep breath and then knocked on the door. In a moment, Deborah answered, surprised to see Joseph back so soon. She invited him in and called Heli and Mary.

Joseph explained, "I prayed for God to show me what to do, and He sent an *angel* to tell me. He repeated exactly what

33

you had said to me, Mary. I believe what you said! I'm sorry I doubted you, but God had to reveal this to me. Mary, I still want you to be my wife!"

With tears in her eyes, Mary said, "Oh, Joseph, of course I will be your wife. God is so good! We just need to trust in Him, and He will lead us every step of the way."

"Yes, Mary. He has, and He will!" said Joseph.

Heli spoke. "Joseph, there's another miracle baby coming in our family. You remember Zacharias and Elizabeth in Jerusalem?"

"Of course. But they don't have a child, and they're pretty old, aren't they?"

"They are old indeed, but…nothing is impossible for God," Heli said with a smile and a wink. "We have decided that Mary will go and visit Elizabeth for a while. We are quite sure that these two babies are both special gifts from God for our people."

Joseph thought for a moment and then said, "Yes, I see that."

Heli continued, "While Mary is away, perhaps you could finish the work on your house so when she returns she can truly be your bride."

Joseph couldn't hide the smile on his face. "I will do my best," he said. He looked at her. "Mary, I love you. God be with you!"

Joseph hugged Mary and both of her parents. "Shalom," he said, and then he left.

Tabitha and Matzo had been watching from the windowsill. "Well, Tabitha," Matzo said, "it looks like I'm going on a trip!"

To be continued tomorrow…

chapter ten
Mary's First Journey

"**H**ave you got Dan ready yet?" cried Heli to his son Ben.

"Yes, I'll be right there!" Ben brought the trusty family donkey to the front of the house.

Heli petted the donkey on the head and whispered into his ear, "Ah, Dan, this is the most important assignment you've ever had! Make sure you keep Mary comfortable—she is carrying something, or some*one,* very precious!"

Deborah and Mary came through the front door. Deborah asked, "Is Uncle Nathan here yet? Or is he late as usual?"

But before Heli could answer, a joyful voice called out from down the road, "Good morning, everyone! Shalom to you, Heli, and your house! May the Lord bless you and keep you!"

Heli's brother, Nathan, rode toward them on his donkey. "And you as well, Nathan!" said Heli in a loud voice. "It is good to see you!" The brothers embraced. Heli continued, "And you are very kind to take my daughter to see cousin Elizabeth. It is a long trip, and she could not make it alone."

"Of course, Heli," said Nathan, "it's my pleasure. And since I have business in Jerusalem anyway, it is really no trouble. I'm also looking forward to seeing Elizabeth. It's been quite some time since I've visited with her and Zacharias. And to imagine that they are having a child—it's a miracle!"

"Yes, it must be!" replied Heli. "And Ben will be going with you. He can bring Dan back so you won't have to deal with him."

"Fine idea," said Nathan. "I look forward to his excellent company!"

They loaded up Dan with Mary and Ben's belongings. Then Ben lifted Mary onto the donkey's back. Uncle Nathan climbed onto his own donkey, and they were ready to go. Heli prayed over the travellers and bade them farewell.

Mary looked down and noticed a small patch of brown fur at the top of one of her bags. She whispered, "Matzo, what are you doing here? You can't come with me!"

Ben looked back and asked, "What did you say?"

Mary said, "Oh, nothing much. I'll tell you later." She smiled at him.

Ben turned his attention back to the road, and Mary looked down at the cute brown face and big brown eyes staring back at her as if to say "Please?"

Mary sighed. "Oh, I guess it's okay. But I don't know what Zacharias will think of a mouse staying in his home."

It was a long way to Jerusalem. It took three days, so there was lots of time for conversation and singing with their uncle. Both Ben and Mary enjoyed Uncle Nathan because of his cheerful personality and the many stories he told them about their father when he was a little boy. He made them laugh hard, and they appreciated every minute with him.

Mary was always excited when she went to Jerusalem, but this time there was an extra thrill as they walked through the outskirts, making their way into the heart of God's city. She, who of all people was carrying a very special child, was going to see her cousin who evidently was also carrying a special child. What could it all mean? What did the future hold?

Matzo had never been to Jerusalem, so he wanted to take it all in: the big buildings, the street vendors, the markets, and the magnificent temple. He had never seen such splendour in his life! He was glad that Uncle Nathan had come along to keep them safe and to guide them through the busy city.

At last they got to Zacharias and Elizabeth's house. Mary's heart was racing as Uncle Nathan helped her get off Dan. What was she going to say? What did Elizabeth know? Would she even understand why Mary was there?

They went to the front door and knocked. A servant opened the door, said, "Shalom," and let them in. As they entered the hallway, Mary said, "Shalom" to the servant. Just then she heard a woman exclaiming, "Oh, my!"

Mary's eyes were already wide with wonder, but they got even wider when Elizabeth, with equally wide eyes, appeared around a corner and said, "Mary—you're here!" Without even greeting the men, she continued, "Wait till I tell you what just happened!"

To be continued tomorrow...

chapter eleven

Settling In

"Tell me what?" asked Mary, surprised by Elizabeth's greeting.

"Mary, as soon as I heard your voice at the door, the baby inside me jumped! I am so blessed to have the mother of my Lord come to visit me." Elizabeth had the widest smile.

Mary shook her head in wonder. She realized that Elizabeth knew much more about her situation than anyone else did. She believed that their babies would be very special children, but what a surprise that a baby in one mother's tummy could respond to another baby! Mary hadn't even felt Jesus moving around inside her yet, but Elizabeth's baby could tell He was extraordinary!

"Mary, do you realize how special you are? God has chosen you to be the mother of the Saviour of the world! You are blessed because you believed the things the Lord told you. Oh my, my…the baby keeps jumping for joy inside me. I feel like I'm on a bumpy camel ride!" exclaimed Elizabeth.

The two women hugged and cried happy tears of joy. Uncle Nathan and Ben didn't quite understand what was going on, but knowing that girls are different than boys, they went to get Mary's things off Dan's back.

Matzo had fallen asleep in one of Mary's bags. He woke up to the sound of Nathan and Ben laughing about Elizabeth saying that she felt like she was on a bumpy camel ride.

Just then Matzo heard his favourite sound in the world. Mary was singing. But he didn't recognize the song, and he strained his ears to hear her over the men's chuckling.

> "*My heart rejoices in the Lord,*
> "*My heart rejoices in my God.*
> "*He has shown His great love*
> "*And His favour to me!*
> "*My heart rejoices in the Lord.*"[10]

Matzo was thrilled to hear this song. Every time Mary sang, it was like a sunny day that was peaceful and happy. She made him think of better things than worrying about whether he'd be caught by Festus or Horatio or whether his stomach was full. He began to see that he was no ordinary mouse. Somehow he got to be part of a big and wonderful plan, and he was excited to be at Elizabeth and Zacharias' house.

But when Ben carried the bag Matzo was in into the house, everything changed. Matzo's eyes were not playing tricks on him. A family cat—a pet, not a stray nuisance outside the house but a cat who made her home inside—was curled up under

Zacharias' chair! Mary had said they were staying until Elizabeth's baby was born. That was three months away!

"Phew," said Matzo, "this could be a long visit!"

Right then, Zacharias picked up his cat, Phoebe, and stroked her. Matzo's fur stood straight up on his back, but then he heard Mary, still singing.

> *"He shows mercy to those who worship Him,*
> *"Holy is His Name."*[11]

Matzo calmed down a little as Ben took him and the bag to the room Mary was to stay in. He found a little crack in the wall and decided to hide there for a few days.

It was almost the Sabbath, and Elizabeth had been preparing the meal before her guests arrived. When it was time for them to sit at the Sabbath table, Elizabeth lit the candles and set steaming bowls of delicious food before everyone. She asked Uncle Nathan to sing the prayers.

Zacharias sat at the head of the table and shut his eyes as everyone else joined in the singing. It was a little odd that Zacharias didn't speak. After all, he was a preacher—a priest. However, everyone was happy to be in his warm and welcoming home and didn't mention it.

When he smelled the delicious food, Matzo couldn't stay away. He crept out of his little crack in the wall, slipped under the door, and followed his nose right to the table.

Phoebe was still under Zacharias' chair, but she opened her eyes and arched her back. So Matzo ran right up Mary's skirt, onto her lap. She choked on her food and tried to cover him up with her shawl.

Zacharias dropped his fork and knife and looked at Mary with wide eyes.

She smiled and then whispered, "I'm sorry, Zacharias. Please, he's mine."

Without making a noise, Zacharias shook the whole table with his silent laughter.

It was a peaceful Sabbath meal after all, and everyone, including Matzo and Phoebe, was well fed.

Maybe the next three months wouldn't feel so long after all.

To be continued tomorrow...

chapter twelve

John Is Born

The time passed quickly for both Mary and Elizabeth. There was much to be done to get ready for the new baby. Elizabeth and Zacharias had been married for many, many years without a child, so a cradle, blankets, diapers, and sleepers had to be made. An angel had told Zacharias that their baby was a boy, just like Mary's, so they made brown and blue curtains instead of pink ones.

It was an exciting time, and Elizabeth was happy to have Mary's company during the last few months of her pregnancy. Zacharias had been unable to talk since the angel announced their baby's coming. He could write messages, and Elizabeth could talk to him, but being able to have conversations with someone was a blessing. God knew she needed that and sent Mary to her. They shared all their excitement for the way their lives were about to change forever.

Finally the day arrived. Zacharias went to the temple, as was his custom. He saw his old friends Simeon and Anna, and as usual he waved to them and spoke with a smile in his eyes rather than with words. Both Anna and Simeon were faithful servants of the Lord who spent their days praying and prophesying about the coming Messiah. Little did they know that a young girl named Mary who was visiting in Zacharias' house would soon give birth to Him! But they believed He would come. Believing is the most important thing.

When Zacharias returned home, he expected to smell his supper cooking. Instead the house was full of steam from pots of boiling water. Something unusual was happening! Soon he realized that his wife was having their baby.

Matzo and Phoebe were both excited. They were curled up *together* outside Elizabeth's room while Mary and other ladies took care of Elizabeth. You see, over the past three months, they had become good friends! Phoebe was not like the other cats Matzo knew. She was a good cat!

Zacharias washed up, and before long he was called to see Elizabeth. The midwife met him with a huge smile. She said, "Zacharias, let me introduce you to your son!"

The Lord had heard their prayers! Their baby boy was born.

Matzo squeaked with delight, and Phoebe purred loudly and happily. That was their way of praising the Lord. The whole household celebrated the baby's birth.

Eight days later, it was time to take the baby to the temple to be dedicated to the Lord. All the neighbours and friends were curious about this child born to the priest Zacharias and his wife. They were old enough to have grandchildren, but God had blessed them with their first son in their old age.

As they walked to the temple, Zacharias thought back to the day, months earlier, when he had been ministering to the

Lord. Suddenly, the angel Gabriel appeared to him and gave him a message from God. He and Elizabeth were to have a son in their old age! Gabriel said that many would rejoice with them at their boy's birth and that the child would be great in the sight of God. He also said that the boy would be filled with the Holy Spirit even while he was still in Elizabeth's tummy. God had a very special plan to use him to help people get ready to receive the Lord! It was all so wonderful that Zacharias asked, "How can I be sure of this?"[12]

Because he had doubted the words that Gabriel spoke, Zacharias was unable to speak for almost an entire year! But God is merciful, and His promise was fulfilled, just as the angel had spoken. And here they were, about to dedicate their son!

In those days, children were named at their dedication. All the people were curious about the priest's new baby, and everyone expected that the child's name would be Zacharias. Usually children were named after their parents.

When the people asked, Elizabeth answered, "His name is John."

The people gasped. Someone asked, "Why would you name him *John*? None of your relatives has that name!" So they gestured to Zacharias, asking for his decision.

Zacharias motioned for a tablet (that's something like a chalkboard) to write on, and he wrote, "His name is John."

No sooner did he get his sentence written than his tongue started to move and he got his voice back! His first words were praise and worship to God. He was filled with the Holy Spirit and began to speak about the ways God would use his son, John, to turn people's hearts toward God. He would help people get ready to receive the Messiah! His child would be great because of the greatness of God in him.

The people of Jerusalem were astonished at what they heard and saw. Some were even a bit frightened because they couldn't understand. They would discuss it at the market and wonder, "What kind of child is this new baby, John?" In their homes everyone talked about old Elizabeth and Zacharias. The "silent preacher" was now prophesying! Things were changing, and people wondered what else was going happen in their lifetime.

While all this was happening in Jerusalem, Mary, Matzo, Ben and Uncle Nathan had returned to Nazareth. New adventures were about to happen for them as well!

To be continued tomorrow…

chapter thirteen

The House Is Finished

"Tabitha," called Joseph as he placed a last shovelful of dirt at the base of the fig tree. "Fly over here and perch in Mary's tree. This is the last detail, and I'm finally done. I think Mary will be home today!"

Tabitha flew gracefully from her windowsill to the new tree. She had watched Joseph work hard on the house from dawn to dusk every day except the Sabbaths for the past three months. The day before, he sanded the doorposts, and today he was finishing the yard. He had even found time to build a beautiful cradle for baby Jesus. He wanted his bride to love her new home.

"What do you think, Tabitha?" Joseph asked with a huge grin on his face.

Tabitha cooed and fluttered her wings to show her approval. Not only was this house beautifully finished for Mary, but Tabitha lived here too, and she thought it was the best home in all of Nazareth.

A week earlier, Joseph had proudly told Heli that the house was almost complete and that Mary could come home whenever her father sent for her. Heli had patted his son-in-law on the back and told him he was thankful that Jehovah had chosen Joseph to be Mary's husband. It was going to take a very special man to be the earthly father of God's Son, the Saviour of the world.

Heli had thought a lot about what it would be like to be Jesus' grampa. Would he be able to teach him the Torah like he had Ben, Mary, Abby and Rachel? He had many questions, and he wanted to know if Joseph had questions too. The Torah told of angels that appeared to Father Abraham and Jacob, and now one had come to his home and to Joseph's. It seemed like a dream in some ways, but in his heart he knew that life was about to change forever and it was all very real.

After Joseph's visit, Heli sent word to Zacharias that the time had come for Mary to return home. Uncle Nathan and Ben would once again travel with her. Zacharias sent word back that Elizabeth had given birth to their son, John, and Mary had been a great blessing to their family. He even mentioned how his cat, Phoebe, and Mary's mouse, Matzo, had become friends. Heli smiled as he thought of his daughter in their cousin's house. He had missed little Matzo, and he was ready to have his girl and her mouse back home.

Mary's mother, Deborah, had been busy planning the wedding celebration with Abby and Rachel. Girls love weddings! They had been preparing food for weeks in anticipation of Joseph finishing the house. The flowers in the garden were ready to be picked for full, fragrant bouquets. The girls had thought more about the wedding celebration than the birth of the baby. But when Mary rode down the lane with Uncle Nathan and Ben, their eyes got wide like saucers when they saw her sitting on Dan with her full, round tummy! Of course, they knew she was having a baby, but she didn't look like it when she left. She appeared different now—beautiful, but different.

Matzo also had a full, round tummy, but for another reason! Elizabeth and Zacharias had fed him too well while he visited them in Jerusalem. They liked having guests, and they shared their food unselfishly. He didn't know if he'd be able to sneak under the crack in Heli's door or would have to walk inside like the rest of the family did! His fur was thick, and his tummy was chubby and full. He had spent three months living like a city mouse and hadn't had to run away from his cat friend Phoebe, who was fed even better than he was!

But now Mary and Matzo were home in Nazareth, ready to soon settle down at Joseph's house. It was good to be back!

To be continued tomorrow...

chapter fourteen

Joseph and Mary

T he wedding was beautiful! Mary was radiant, and Joseph was overjoyed with his new bride and his new family. Heli and Deborah had prepared everything superbly, so the ceremony gave great glory to God and also brought great honour to both Mary and Joseph. The family and friends who came for the special occasion were treated to the best hospitality, and they were all glad they had made the trip. It was quite simply a perfect day!

But that was yesterday, and now Joseph and Mary were busy settling into their new home. But this was a different kind of "busy" for Joseph. He was used to his carpentry work and house-building, but according to Jewish law, the groom was to take a year off work after his wedding. So there was no carpentry for Joseph, and no house building! But he was very pleased to spend his days with his beautiful bride, making their house into a cozy home.

They walked around their new house and stopped at the beautiful fig tree Joseph had planted. It was very special to

Mary. It reminded her of God's faithfulness and His tender care for her people.

They had noticed an unusual number of Roman soldiers around Nazareth, and Mary asked Joseph what it meant. But he didn't know. "I can't imagine it means anything good, but we have to live with them." They continued walking, talking about the new house and property. Soon they forgot about the soldiers.

Matzo was also settling in. He spent some time looking for the perfect spot for his new nest. He searched high and low, and one place really caught his eye. Right up by the windowsill where Tabitha made her nest, Matzo noticed a little hollow in the wall that would be perfect for him.

But there was a problem. Matzo was used to living with a family, with people coming and going, all the while sharing everything they had. But Tabitha had been alone with Joseph, and he was at work most of the time. She wasn't used to people being around so much. And she certainly wasn't used to sharing her windowsill with anyone!

When Matzo asked her if he could build his nest up beside hers, she got flustered and started crying. Joseph and Mary heard all the commotion and came to see what was happening. At first they didn't understand what was wrong, but then Joseph saw what was bothering Tabitha.

He said gently, "Tabitha, my dear, we have lived alone here for a long time, but now our family is getting bigger. We have to learn to make room for others in our lives. I am learning to share with Mary, and you will have to learn to share with Pipsqueak." He winked at Matzo.

Mary said, "Joseph, if Tabitha isn't ready to share her windowsill with Matzo, that's okay. This is all new for her."

But wise Joseph said, "I know things are changing, but when God does something special in our lives, we have to learn to accept it. Today, God has made our lives much bigger with you and Matzo joining us. We rejoice in what He has done, and we will make room! Mary, I know how Tabitha feels, but you wouldn't want me to act that way toward you, would you?" He smiled broadly and gave her a tender kiss.

Blushing slightly, Mary said, "Yes, you're right. I just don't want her to feel like Matzo is an intruder."

"She will get used to it," said Joseph, "as will I." He winked and smiled again.

Tabitha understood. While it took some self-control, she welcomed Matzo into her home and her life. Matzo found lots of sawdust and woodchips to make a perfect nest near hers. The two of them made a pretty cute picture on their little windowsill.

It took some work on everyone's part, but they learned to live together happily. They all knew very well that it was God's plan, and so there was also plenty of God's grace for each of them—even a mouse and a turtledove!

To be continued tomorrow...

chapter fifteen

Soldiers Come Calling

The days turned into weeks, and the weeks turned into months. Joseph and Mary loved one another and were growing closer and stronger as the time passed. They enjoyed their peaceful home and were determined to please God with their lives.

Matzo and Tabitha also grew closer, learning to share and get along. Tabitha grew to be thankful for Matzo. She realized how important it was to have a good friend.

BANG, BANG, BANG! A loud smashing sound came from the front door. BANG, BANG, BANG! Joseph and Mary rushed to the door, and Matzo's fur stood up on his back. After looking at Mary with concern in his eyes, Joseph opened the door.

Three Roman soldiers stood outside. One was on their doorstep, facing them with his sword in his hand. He had used the large gleaming weapon to make the banging sound on their door. Two others soldiers, behind him on either side, looked straight ahead.

"You live here?" growled the man on the step.

"Yes, I do," said Joseph calmly.

The soldier looked at him sternly. "There's a meeting today at noon in the town square. Caesar Augustus requires all residents to attend."

"What is it about?" asked Joseph.

"I guess you'll find out when you get there, won't you?" snapped the soldier.

"I suppose we will," said Joseph.

Just then Matzo heard a sound that made his blood freeze. It was a low, long, whining "meeeeeeeooooow" coming from just outside the door. Standing by Mary's feet, he looked out and couldn't believe his eyes! Festus and Horatio were standing beside the two rear soldiers. It looked as if they were part of the group! As Matzo stared, Festus noticed him and fixed his eyes on him. Matzo was too scared to move.

Suddenly Festus darted toward the door, trying to get to Matzo. But just as suddenly, the front soldier's foot swung out and kicked him solidly, sending him flying. Matzo scurried up to his nest in the windowsill where he could keep an eye on the cats without being seen (or so he thought).

"What do you mean by that nonsense, you mangy beast?" the soldier shouted. He then looked at Joseph and said, "Today at noon!"

"Today at noon," replied Joseph.

The front soldier turned around and marched away, followed by the two other soldiers and then Festus and Horatio. Festus was limping a bit, but he turned around and, looking straight up at Matzo in the windowsill, gave a long meow. Matzo shivered.

Joseph looked at his front door. He had worked hard to give it a beautiful smooth finish. But now he saw scratches and gouges made by the hilt of the soldier's sword. "Those inconsiderate—" He was going to say something in anger, but he held his tongue.

Mary asked, "Joseph, what does this mean? What do they want?"

"I don't know," said Joseph. "But our trust is in God, my dear, and He will take care of us no matter what we face."

Matzo could see some fear in Tabitha's eyes, but as they looked at one another they were encouraged by Joseph's words. "Don't worry, Tabitha. Nothing is impossible for God! We'll be fine," said Matzo.

Mary and Joseph now needed to make preparations for attending the meeting in a little over two hours.

To be continued tomorrow…

chapter sixteen

The Roman Decree

A huge clap of thunder shook all the people walking to the town square. The lightning seemed far away, but the boom that quickly followed made everyone gasp with fright. Then rain began to fall. It was a full downpour, not a light trickle.

By the time Joseph and Mary arrived at the town square they were soaking wet. Mary's veil clung to her brow, and Joseph's drenched robe revealed a thin but strong man underneath. Tabitha had been flying overhead, but when the lightning struck she flew down onto Joseph's shoulder. Matzo ran from behind. Puddles that seemed as big as ponds quickly developed on the rough road, and he began to choke as water filled his eyes and lungs.

Whatever Caesar wanted couldn't wait. The soldiers had been to everyone's houses, pounding with their heavy swords and spears on the villagers' doors. Joseph's nearest neighbours complained that Roman horses had run through their yard, destroying the vegetable patch. Usually the horses were very disciplined, but the nasty weather and angry soldiers made even them nervous today.

Joseph and Mary trudged to the centre of town. Heli and Deborah and the children, who were all soaking wet, looked concerned. But the sight of family put a smile on everyone's faces. They reached each other and gave hugs and kisses to all.

At that moment a large and frightening captain of the Roman army appeared on the platform in the centre of the square. He called out over the pelting rain, "Hear ye, hear ye! I come to you today in the name of Caesar Augustus. Within the next two weeks, every man and his household must return to his city of birth and be registered with the Roman tax office!"

A groan arose from the crowd.

"There will be no exceptions," the officer continued. "Appear in the town of your father's birth or be prepared to lose your home and property!"

Lose their home and property! Who did these Romans think they were to make such a demand?

As the crowd murmured and grumbled the soldier raised his voice again. "Silence! I said, silence! You have heard the decree! You have two weeks. There are no exceptions! Failure to obey will result in dire consequences."

The crowd was silent...except for a high-pitched squeak from a drenched mouse. Matzo had finally made it to the town square. His voice caught the attention of Mary, Joseph and Tabitha. But that's not all; the ears of two wet and nasty cats perked up!

Matzo was hoping his family would recognize his voice. He wasn't thinking about the cats. Even though Festus and Horatio had been adopted by a soldier named Balbus and had

regular meals, they still wanted to get the little mouse. They followed the sound of his voice.

"Pipsqueak!" whispered Joseph. "Why did you leave the house?"

Matzo's eyes were wet with rain, but it also looked like he was crying. He had been frightened by the thunder and the loud voices of the captain of the army, and he just wanted his family.

"There, there," said Mary quietly. She was having a hard time bending over to pick him up because her tummy was so big. As she reached down, Festus darted through the crowd and plucked him up by the scruff of the neck! He began to run away with Matzo in his mouth.

Seeing all this from above, Tabitha got a burst of courage. As another clap of thunder sounded, she swooped down and poked Festus between the eyes with her beak. The cat squawked and dropped Matzo in a puddle.

Joseph scooped Matzo up as a Roman soldier called out, "What's all the commotion?" Joseph stood and faced the soldier. "You have heard the decree. Make preparations to return to your father's hometown. Immediately!"

Matzo's little heart beat faster than the raindrops fell. Festus nursed his poked nose. Tabitha felt like she had just done a heroic deed, and Joseph gathered his family. "Let's get home," he said quietly.

The crowd dispersed. As they walked slowly down the wet, muddy street, Joseph put his arm around Mary's shoulder to reassure her.

Mary patted her stomach and sighed. "Baby Jesus, it looks like we are taking another journey. This time we'll go beyond Jerusalem to Bethlehem. Oh, when and where will You be born, little One?"

To be continued tomorrow...

chapter seventeen

The Preparations Begin

Heli and Deborah followed Joseph and Mary home. They were all dripping wet and stunned by the news. Mary put the kettle on the woodstove and prepared some biscuits and cheese to eat. No one said much as they thought about one more change that was coming to their family.

Deborah sighed under her breath, "When Messiah comes, He will rid us of all our enemies!" Then she looked over at Mary and thought of the little baby inside her. *How can that little baby save our people from these Roman tyrants?* She wasn't the only one wondering the same thing, but none of them spoke.

Heli looked at Mary, who stood over the stove, and thought that she still looked like a little girl from the back. Then she turned around, and he saw her full tummy. He thought, *My little girl is now a momma herself. I know she and Joseph will be able to face their future with God's help.*

Mary said, "The tea is ready. Momma, can you help me serve, please? I'm a little awkward, and I don't want to spill anything and get anyone wet!"

This little joke broke the silence, and they all laughed. They were already soaked! Then they began to all talk at once.

"Will you take the baby's clothes with you on your journey?" asked Abigail.

"How much food do you need to take with you?" asked Ben.

"You may have Dan for the journey, Joseph," offered Heli. "He's used to having Mary on his back, and he is a trustworthy animal for such important travellers!"

"Do you think Dan is strong enough for *her?*" joked Ben as he pointed to Mary's big tummy.

Mary slapped Ben on the head with her tea towel and said, "I think I could still beat you in an arm wrestle, little brother!"

"You're on!" smiled Ben as he stood up, flexing his muscles.

"Hey, wait, you two," interrupted Joseph. "Ben, I'll take you on in Mary's place!"

Ben decided to surrender, and the family enjoyed their tea and biscuits and then got to the business of planning Joseph and Mary's journey.

Meanwhile, Matzo and Tabitha were making arrangements of their own. Matzo's neck was a little raw from Festus' teeth, but he forgot about that soon enough. He had learned to appreciate his friend Tabitha, and today she had saved his life!

"Tabitha, what can I do to repay you?" he asked in a squeaky emotional voice.

"Let's just stick together," said Tabitha. "There may be a few more struggles ahead of us, and we're going to need each other." She paused for a moment. "I never thought I'd be saying this to you, Matzo, but when I saw you in Festus' mouth, I couldn't bear to think of being without you. Turtledoves aren't exactly used to fighting Roman cats, but I guess you could say, 'Nothing is impossible for God!'" She smiled and continued, "And I know that today He helped me to save you."

"Thank you! We'll make this journey together, Tabitha," said Matzo. "I've been to Jerusalem before, but we have to go even farther, to Bethlehem. We'll be there for each other, and we'll be there for Joseph, Mary and the baby."

The day had begun with a loud banging on the door, but it ended peacefully. Heli and Deborah prayed for Joseph and Mary and committed their journey and preparations to the Lord. They hugged each other and said goodbye for the night. They all needed to rest because the next few days would be busy!

To be continued tomorrow...

chapter eighteen

Joseph and Mary Leave Nazareth

Deborah looked over the supplies Joseph was packing. "Mary, I don't think you have enough food, darling!" she worried.

"Oh, Momma," said Mary, "we'll be fine. We have enough for many days, and there are plenty of villages and towns; we can buy more if we need it."

"But Mimi, you're eating for two now—you have to keep your strength up!" said Deborah, trying to convince them. She wanted to say more, but she could see that Joseph thought they had enough to eat. And she had learned that when Joseph made his mind up, it was made up!

Just then, Abby and Rachel came in. "We made you two more swaddling cloths," said Abby as she put them in Mary's pack.

Joseph asked, "Swaddling cloths? What are swaddling cloths?"

Rachel rolled her eyes, "Don't you know anything? They're for wrapping up a baby to keep him warm and still."

Joseph smiled. "Well, I guess I still have some learning to do! But Abby, we should be back in less than two weeks. We hope to have the baby here after we've returned. But I suppose you never know exactly when a baby will come, do you?"

"You sure don't!" said Abby. "Don't you remember Mrs. Solomon's third child, Hephzibah? She came *five weeks* before they expected her!"

Deborah turned and said, "Yes, but this is Mary's *first*, not her third. And first babies don't often come early."

Heli came into the room with a smile on his face. He said, "No, first babies don't often come early. But I was reading something interesting from the Torah this morning. The prophet Micah says, 'Bethlehem Ephrath, you are one of the smallest towns in the nation of Judah. But the LORD will choose one of your people to rule the nation—someone whose family goes back to ancient times.'"[13]

Everyone started whispering.

"The One?"

"Bethlehem?"

"Ruler over Judah?"

"What does all this mean?"

Heli said, "I don't know exactly what it means." He look at Mary and continued, "But, my dear, you and Joseph had better be ready for anything."

The front door burst open, and Ben walked in. He announced loudly, "Dan is ready! We can start loading him up. I tried riding him this morning along with two of my friends—all of us on him at the same time—and he was still able to walk. So

I think he should be able to hold my *big* sister!" He put his hands around his tummy as if he weighed 400 pounds.

Everyone laughed, and then they took the packs outside to the donkey. While it was a joyful time, Heli and Deborah were a little quieter than usual. They knew that their beautiful daughter and her husband were courageously doing exactly what God had told them to do. But they also didn't know when they would see them or their grandchild next.

Heli whispered to Deborah, "Our trust is in God!"

She replied, "Yes, Heli, our trust *is* in God!"

Joseph picked up Mary's bag and saw a little patch of brown fur inside. "Pipsqueak," he said, "do you think you're coming too?" Matzo looked up with his big brown eyes.

Mary said, "Well, Joseph, you said you're going to bring Tabitha, and the two of them have been sticking together like glue recently."

"Yes, I suppose you're right." Joseph chuckled. "Let's get you all aboard now. We do have to be off soon or we'll miss too much daylight, and I don't want to travel at night."

They loaded Dan with all the packs, and then, after Mary hugged everyone in her family, Joseph lifted her onto the donkey's back. She was used to riding him, so she was comfortable enough. Tabitha flew over and perched on Joseph's shoulder.

Joseph embraced Heli. The older man looked him in the eye and said, "Take good care of her—and *Him!* God be with you."

"Thank you, Heli. God *is* indeed with us. Immanuel!"

The young family started down the roadway toward Bethlehem. Heli and Deborah watched them go—Joseph walking, Mary riding on Dan, Tabitha on Joseph's shoulder, and little Matzo on Mary's lap.

"God be with you," repeated Heli as he put his arms around Deborah and the children.

To be continued tomorrow...

chapter nineteen

On the Road to Bethlehem

J oseph recited Scripture under his breath as he led Dan the donkey along the road. This trip was about more than registering in the tax office in Bethlehem. There was a bigger plan, and the only thing he knew to do was to trust God, who had already brought angels to help in the past months.

Mary too was deep in thought. Suddenly the babe inside her started to kick! Matzo, who was sitting on her lap, felt it too. He looked at Mary as if to ask, what was that?

Mary looked down at Matzo and laughed. "I think baby Jesus wants to make sure we're on the right road. He's kicking us both!" She paused and then said, "Oh, Matzo, what do you think He'll be like? Do you think I'll be a good momma to Him?"

Matzo squeaked back to Mary, and Joseph joined the conversation. "What's up, Pipsqueak? Did you see Festus and Horatio in the ditch?"

Mary replied, "No, Joseph, but our baby is letting us know that He's got feet strong enough to kick a soccer ball!"

"So He's kicking, is He? Do you think He'll ever play for the Nazareth Nomads?" teased Joseph.

"If He wants to, I'm sure his Uncle Ben will coach Him!" Mary chuckled, and then she let out a squeal. The baby kicked her right in the ribs, and she had to grab Dan's mane so she didn't fall off his back! Matzo, however, couldn't find anything to hang on to, and he tumbled right off Mary's lap and onto the rough road. No one noticed that he was gone, because they were talking, laughing and joking about baby Jesus playing soccer.

Matzo squeaked as loudly as his little lungs could blast as he watched his family move on ahead of him down the road, but they didn't hear him.

Sheep grazing in the field beside the path called out to Matzo. "Baa, baa, wh-wh-where are you all heading with such a b-b-big l-l-l-load?"

Matzo peeped back, "We are off to Bethlehem. My family is from the house of David—you know, the great shepherd king. We are going to register at the tax office."

"Wh-wh-whaaaat's a tax office?" asked a woolly sheep.

"I don't know, but it can't be good. The Roman soldiers said that Caesar wants to count everyone. Something to do with money—that's all I know," replied Matzo.

"Sounds pretty baaaaad!" answered a sheep.

"I think it is," squealed Matzo, "but I have to go! Look, my family is down the road, and they don't even know where I am. See you in a few weeks. And we're going to have a new baby by then!"

"A b-b-baaaby? We thought b-b-b-baaaabies were b-b-b-born in the s-s-s-spring, not in the winter!" bleated the sheep.

"Well, animal babies are often born in the spring, but I think people babies can be born anytime. Anyway, I gotta go!" And off ran Matzo down the lane.

Tabitha had noticed that Matzo was gone, and she was flying overhead, watching out for her little friend. The donkey with his heavy load wasn't moving quickly, so in a few minutes Matzo caught up.

When Mary saw Matzo she scolded him for running off— it could be dangerous for him. She didn't realize that he hadn't *run* off; he'd been *kicked* off!

Down the crooked road the family travelled until it was time to find a place to stop for the night. As the sky grew dark, they noticed a bright gleaming star close to where they were headed.

To be continued tomorrow...

chapter twenty

Jericho

The first few days of Joseph and Mary's journey toward Bethlehem passed without too many surprises. Joseph had made the trip to Jerusalem every year at Passover since he was a boy, so he knew the route well, along with all the good places to stay for the night.

As they came toward Jericho, Mary and Joseph decided to recite the story of how Joshua and the children of Israel had marched around that city for six days. Then on the seventh day, after marching seven times, blowing horns and shouting, they saw the walls fall. Joseph couldn't help himself; he started to march—left, right, left, right—as they walked on the dusty Jericho road. They talked about Joshua and all the things he had done as he led God's people.

When Joseph said Joshua's name in Hebrew—*Yehoshua*, which means "God is salvation," Mary whispered the name the angel had told her to call their baby—*Yeshua*, which means "salvation." Joshua had led the children of Israel into the Promised Land—into their salvation. Joseph remembered the words the angel said to him: "After the baby is born, name him Jesus, because he will save his people from their sins."[14] And Joseph's great-great-great-great-grandmother Rahab had hidden the two spies, and then she herself was saved by Joshua.

They had so much to think about! They retold the stories they had known from their childhood. They thought of the great miracles that the children of Israel had seen—the plagues in Egypt, the splitting of the Red Sea, and the walls of Jericho tumbling to the ground.

Suddenly they were interrupted by loud, angry voices. "Stop in the name of Caesar Augustus, the mighty emperor of the Roman world!"

Joseph said, "Whoa," and he and Dan came to a stop. Mounted soldiers blocked their way, with swords and shields gleaming in the sunlight.

The scene was a picture of opposites. Little Mary was sitting on rugged old Dan with her faithful husband at her side. The soldiers were riding strong, tall horses. Joseph wore a Jewish skullcap, also called a kippah, on the top of his head, while the soldiers wore huge metal helmets with bird feathers that had been dyed bright red. The soldiers looked familiar to Joseph, but he wasn't sure why.

One of them got off his horse and came closer to Joseph with a strange expression on his face. He took his sword out of its sheath, raised it, and pointed it straight at Joseph's face. He slowly brought it toward him.

Joseph hadn't done anything wrong, but he didn't dare move. Mary sat up nervously. She wanted to reach out and grab the sword, but she also knew that she must not budge. They could both feel their hearts pounding in their chests.

Closer and closer the sword came to Joseph as sweat began to build up on his brow. As it came just close enough to touch him, the soldier tapped Tabitha off his shoulder with it! She flew into the air and circled overhead.

The soldier said, "That turtledove of yours could get a shekel or two from some of the vendors in Jerusalem. They're always selling birds for some sacrifice or another."

Both Joseph and Mary let out a deep sigh of relief. The soldier was more interested in the bird than in Joseph.

Matzo squeaked loudly, and who should appear from under the soldiers' breastplates but Festus and Horatio! It was as though they had followed Matzo all the way from Nazareth. Festus let out a loud "Meeeooowww," squinted his eyes and hissed at Matzo.

Matzo hid underneath Mary's shawl and shook like a leaf. It was then that Joseph recognized the soldier as Balbus, who had adopted the two cats.

Sacrifice! thought Tabitha as she flew around. *I'm glad I'm not a candidate, since I broke my wing last spring. Phew!* You see, to be a sacrifice, animals had to have no injuries or blemishes—they had to be perfect.

Joseph answered, "My bird is far from perfect. She's just a good pet, not worthy to be used as an offering for sin."

"Offering for sin!" grumbled the soldier. "What could ever pay for sin? Surely we're stuck with it forever!"

Joseph said, "The Messiah will come, and He will save us all from our sins."

Just then Mary felt her baby jumping in her tummy, as if He was saying, "And I am coming sooner than they think!"

The soldier replied, "Whatever! Now get on with you! You have a deadline to meet, and it looks like you might be having a baby during your travels."

Matzo shook, and Tabitha flew overhead. She didn't want to get anywhere near that soldier's sword again.

Joseph returned to his marching while Dan carried Mary and Matzo down the dusty Jericho road.

To be continued tomorrow...

chapter twenty-one

The Valley of the Shadow of Death

Matzo didn't sleep well that night. They had found a comfortable inn with good food, but he dreamt about soldiers, horses, swords, and, well, cats— Festus and Horatio in particular. He dreamt about their green eyes and their yellow teeth, and he kept waking up, thinking he heard their low meows outside the window. But he knew it was a dream.

He could hardly believe that the two cats had travelled to exactly the same place as Joseph and Mary had. How could that be? He also thought about the beautiful bright star they had seen again, as they had every night of their trip. It almost seemed to be pointing to their destination.

When the family woke up in the morning, they had their devotions and prayer. Then, after a good breakfast, they started on their journey again. The early hours were quite cool, but the sun was shining in a beautiful blue sky.

They travelled along the well-worn road, but soon Joseph turned off onto a smaller path. "This way is shorter than the main road," he said. "And we don't have any time to spare."

"Is it safe?" asked Mary.

"Yes, it is safe, but we won't find many others along this way," replied Joseph. "And it should be free of any Roman soldiers!"

"Where will it take us?" asked Mary.

"Through a valley."

"Does the valley have a name?" asked Mary.

"Well, I have heard some people call it the valley of the shadow of death," said Joseph quietly.

"Tabitha!" squeaked Matzo. "Did you hear that? *The valley of the shadow of death?* I sure hope it's safe!"

Tabitha replied, "If Joseph said it's safe, then you can be sure it's safe. He would never lead Mary astray. You can trust him."

Joseph, almost as if he had understood the two animals, said, "Mary, there is nothing to fear. Do you remember the twenty-third psalm?"

"The Lord is my shepherd?" she asked.

"Yes, that's the one. Do you remember who wrote it?"

"Your great-great-great-grandfather, King David!"

"Yes, that's right. Let's recite it." So they said together, "The LORD is my shepherd, I shall not want. He makes me lie down in green pastures. He leads me beside still waters. He restores my soul. He leads me in paths of righteousness for his name's sake. Even though I walk through the valley of the shadow of death, I will fear no evil, for you are with me; your rod and your staff, they comfort me."[15]

"See," cooed Tabitha, "I told you we're going to be safe!"

"You prepare a table before me in the presence of my enemies."[16]

"Yes, I believe we'll be safe," said Matzo, "but I sure am getting hungry!"

"You anoint my head with oil; my cup overflows. Surely goodness and mercy shall follow me all the days of my life, and I shall dwell in the house of the LORD forever."[17]

Mary said, "It's such a wonderful psalm. He wrote beautifully, didn't he?"

"Yes, he did." Joseph paused. "I've been thinking about David a lot lately. Do you remember the Scripture in Isaiah that says 'to us a child is born, to us a son is given'?"[18]

Mary replied, "I've heard it, but what does that Scripture have to do with David?"

"Well, the next verse says that he, the son who is born, will rule with fairness and justice from the throne of his ancestor David *forever*."

Mary said, "Forever! Israel has had so many kings over the years. Who could rule forever?"

Just then, baby Jesus kicked again—and kicked, and kicked! Again Mary held on to Dan's mane, but Matzo was knocked off her lap and down onto the sand. As he scampered up Dan's leg and back onto Mary's lap, he heard Joseph say, "I suppose the Son of God will rule forever."

Mary exclaimed, "Oh, Joseph, what an important job God has for us!"

"And us, too!" said Matzo and Tabitha at the same time. Of course, all Joseph and Mary heard was some cooing and squeaking.

Joseph said, "It's the most important job I can imagine! But He is with us every day. He is our Shepherd, and He will guide us every step of the way."

Soon they stopped for lunch, which made Matzo very happy! Then the young family got back on the trail and walked along in silence through the valley toward Jerusalem and new adventures.

To be continued tomorrow...

chapter twenty-two

Jerusalem!

This was Tabitha's first visit to Jerusalem. As they got closer to the eastern gate, she got more and more excited. She had never seen such large buildings and walls—it was beautiful!

Hundreds of other families were going back to their hometowns to be registered. And now as their family entered through the gate into the city, they saw thousands! It was filled with people of all sorts, wearing different kinds of clothes and hats. Tabitha loved hats! She loved flying up and looking at the things people wore on their heads. Of course, she got a different view than the others because she could see the *tops* of the hats! Some were big, small, round, square, triangular, red, blue, gold, silver, brown, plain, jewelled, beaded—just beautiful! She had never seen so many different kinds of hats!

Suddenly she heard Joseph's unmistakable voice calling, "Tabitha! Tabitha!" She wanted to keep flying so she could enjoy the sights, but she knew she had to listen to Joseph, so she flew down and perched on his shoulder.

Joseph said, "Now listen, everyone, we must stay together here in Jerusalem. There are so many people here, it would be easy to get lost if we are separated."

Matzo looked up at Tabitha and said, "Listen to Joseph—don't go flying all over the place!"

Tabitha said, "I won't, but you'd better hang on tight. I've seen you fall off Mary's lap more than once!"

The marketplace was filled with people selling everything imaginable. And it was crowded! People were squished on every side, pushing and bumping each other. Matzo hung on as tightly as he could. He had wrapped his little hands around a few strands of Dan's mane, and although he lost his balance a few times, he kept hanging on.

Suddenly a Roman soldier and his horse pressed through the crowd. People yelled and pushed to get out of the way. "Clear the way!" cried the soldier.

Dan jerked to the right as he was pushed by another donkey trying to get out of the way. Taken by surprise, Matzo couldn't hang on any longer. He went tumbling down onto the muddy street.

As he looked up to find Dan, he saw a horse's hoof coming down right toward him! He let out a squeal and ran as fast as he could. He heard a *thump*, and when he looked back he saw the hoof smash the ground right where he had been a second before. That was close!

Then he looked to his right and saw another hoof—this time belonging to a mule—headed right for him! He ran again. Suddenly he realized that he had no idea where he was.

He looked around to see if Joseph and Mary were nearby but couldn't find them anywhere.

Matzo was afraid. "What if they can't find me? What if I'm lost in Jerusalem? What will I do?" But then he remembered what Joseph and Mary said the day before: "Even though I walk through the valley of the shadow of death, I will fear no evil, for you are with me."[19] He remembered that he could always trust in God, and he calmed down.

Just then he heard a familiar cooing sound from overhead. He looked up and saw Tabitha circling above him. She had spotted him and was signalling Joseph. Very soon, he heard Joseph's voice. "Matzo—are you all right?" Joseph bent down to pick him up. He was fine, but a little dirty. "We thought we had lost you! Thank God Tabitha kept her eye on you!"

Matzo was very grateful. "Thank you, Tabitha—I can always count on you!" he said.

Right then they noticed that Joseph was looking beyond them with wide eyes. In their running and searching, they hadn't noticed where they were, but right behind them was the enormous and beautiful temple of God. They all stopped and stared. Everyone except Tabitha had seen it before, but it was still magnificent and breathtaking every time they saw it.

Joseph said, "Let's go nearer so we can be close to the presence of the Lord."

They walked through a gate into the courtyard surrounding the temple. They couldn't take their eyes off the stunning building. It meant more to them now than it ever had before— God with us!

An old man walked up to them and said to Joseph, "I take it you are going to Bethlehem." Their eyes opened wide. They were all very surprised—how did he know?

Joseph asked, "Who are you?"

"I am a servant of God Most High. I live here, waiting on Him. He has told me of things that are soon going to happen." He fixed his eyes on Mary and said, "Messiah is coming!"

They stood there in stunned silence.

Joseph asked, "How do you know this?"

With gleaming eyes the old man said, "The prophet Amos said, 'The Sovereign LORD never does anything until he reveals his plans to his servants the prophets.'"[20]

Before they could respond, he looked over to his left and called out, "Anna—come here!"

An old woman hobbled toward them. She had bright eyes, a joyful face and a long grey braid running down her back.

"Wonderful! Wonderful!" she said. "When the fullness of time comes, God will send His Son. What a blessing! He has promised that we would see it, Simeon, and He always keeps His promises! Nothing is impossible for God!"

"Yes," said Simeon, "nothing is impossible for God!" Then he told Joseph and Mary, "You'd best be on your way—time is short, you know. You may have a hard time finding a place to stay in Bethlehem. We will see you again soon."

Anna and Simeon turned and disappeared in the crowd. Joseph and Mary could hardly believe what they had just heard. But it was almost mid-afternoon, and it would take two hours to get to Bethlehem. They all wanted to stay a little longer in

Jerusalem!

Jerusalem—there was so much to see—but Simeon was right; they needed to get moving. So they pushed their way through the crowds and out the Zion Gate, which leads toward Bethlehem. Soon they were on the road again, along with many other families.

Joseph prayed, "O Lord, please help us find a place to stay in Bethlehem tonight!"

To be continued tomorrow…

chapter twenty-three

Arrival in Bethlehem

The journey from Jerusalem to Bethlehem took longer than expected, three hours instead of two. The road was bumpy and muddy, a lot of other families were travelling, and Dan wasn't as young as he used to be. He had to stop every half hour or so to drink and rest. Joseph knew he couldn't push the donkey any faster, but he was concerned for Mary. She was getting less talkative and more serious.

Even before the sun set, they all saw the beautiful bright star ahead of them, gleaming in the sky. And when it was dark, the star seemed even bigger and brighter than usual—almost alive, as if it were dancing in the sky.

As they came over the top of a hill, they saw Bethlehem, the city of David. It looked peaceful, even though many people were flowing into it to be registered.

By the time they got into the town, they were all hungry, tired and cold. As they moved along, Joseph, Matzo and Tabitha kept their eyes out for a good place to stay. They looked and looked, but everything was full. Joseph knew it was going to be busy, but arriving earlier would have made this part easier.

For the first time, Joseph felt worried. Mary furrowed her brow from time to time, and he sensed that something was happening with the baby. He asked, "Mary, what is it—what's happening?"

Mary said quietly, "Everything is fine, Joseph, but we need to find a place to stay soon."

"I know. I'm looking, but I don't see anything. We've arrived too late!" Joseph wished he could take those words back—he didn't want to worry Mary.

Mary smiled at Joseph. "Don't worry, dearest. Nothing is impossible for God." She put her hands on her tummy. "And God is with us!"

Joseph was very encouraged. He knew he had to trust God, who had always provided everything they needed. He prayed quietly, "Thank You, Lord, for Your faithfulness. I ask You to provide a place for us to stay tonight. This is such an important time! I thank You, my God."

"Matzo, Tabitha," he said, "let's split up and look for an inn. Matzo, you go south, and Tabitha, you go to the north. I will continue straight ahead. Don't be long, but if you find something, get back right away and let me know."

Tabitha flew off to the north. She could move a lot faster than the others, so she expected to find something quickly. But every place that she saw was full. So she kept going farther to the north and was soon getting close to the edge of the town.

Matzo went, as Joseph told him, to the south. He was slower than Tabitha but faster than Dan. Yet he couldn't find any place for them to stay. He kept running, always keeping track of where he was and remembering where he could find Joseph.

Joseph led Dan on as quickly as he could. Like the others, he could not find anything open for visitors.

Suddenly Mary said, "Joseph, we must find a place now! The baby is coming soon!"

"We will, my dear!" he replied. He looked to his left and saw an inn he hadn't noticed a minute before. Something told him he should go and knock on the door. So he left Mary and Dan to do just that.

When the innkeeper came to the door, Joseph asked if there was a room. "No, we've been full since about six o'clock—sorry!" The man started to shut the door.

Joseph held the door open and said, "But there *must* be a place for us. My wife is going to have a baby soon!"

"A *baby?* Why on earth are you travelling now? Oh, of course, the Roman decree. I'm sorry, but I don't have a place for you. We're all—wait a minute. Well, there is one place you could stay, but it's not very nice. It's where we keep animals. But you could find some clean straw and make a comfortable bed. That's all I can do!"

"We'll take it!" said Joseph. Right then, he heard Mary's voice. "Joseph, please!"

The innkeeper showed them to an opening in a rock wall where he had built a small ceiling and some walls. It wasn't much, but it did offer some shelter from the cool night air.

Joseph found some clean straw and made a bed. Then he helped Mary off Dan's back and carried her over to the straw.

Mary looked at him, and he knew that this was the time they had been waiting for. The birth of their son—God's Son!

Joseph said, "Mary, I am here with you, and God is here. Tell me what to do, and with His help, we shall see a miracle tonight!"

Matzo was still looking when suddenly he knew he needed to go to Mary. So he ran back to the place where they had split up and turned west to follow the way Joseph had gone. He scurried as fast as his little legs could carry him. He looked for Dan but couldn't find him outside any of the inns.

Where are they? he wondered. Just then he heard Mary's voice calling out loudly, "Joseph, oh, Joseph!"

Matzo followed the sound and found Dan, but where was Mary? He heard her voice again, and when he looked, he saw what looked like a barn or a cave. He thought, *Where are they?*

And when he went to the door, he looked in and saw the most beautiful, glorious sight he had ever seen!

To be continued tomorrow…

chapter twenty-four

The Shepherds

Tabitha kept flying north, looking for a place for Joseph and Mary to stay. Once she swooped down low to get a closer look, and she overheard someone say to a traveller, "There's nothing available anymore. You'll have to look out in the country."

Oh dear! Tabitha thought. *Joseph didn't want me to go too far, but that man said to look in the country. If I fly as fast as I can, I'll be able to look around and be back with the rest of them in a few minutes.* She flew higher and faster, north into the open country.

Even though it was dark, she could make out some of the farmhouses and fields. Soon she saw a group of men sitting around a fire in a pasture. She flew closer to see if there was a place to stay nearby. A flock of sheep was close to them, and she realized they were shepherds. She thought, *I didn't realize these guys stay out all night long. I hope they have lots of wood for that fire, or they're going to get cold.*

Suddenly a brilliant light came from above Tabitha. The shepherds looked up, squinting because it was so bright. Tabitha landed on the ground near them and looked up as well. She could hardly believe her eyes—an angel was standing in the sky above them! He looked like the angel she had seen a few months before, shining like the sun, and so very beautiful! He lit up the whole field as if it were noontime. His enormous wings flapped very slowly, and he had a joyful smile on his face.

The shepherds had not seen an angel before, so they were frightened. They didn't know what to do!

And then Tabitha heard it—that powerful rich voice she had heard in Joseph's bedroom when the angel spoke to him.

"Don't be afraid," the angel said. "I'm here to tell you wonderful news! And this news is not for you only but for everyone."

The shepherds stood still, with their eyes focused on the magnificent creature that stood in the sky above them. One of them said softly, "It's an angel!"

"A special child has been born this evening in the city of David—Bethlehem. And this child will be your Saviour, who is Christ the Lord, the Anointed One."

The shepherds were confused. "A Saviour?"

"Christ?"

"A child?"

The angel continued, "This is what you're to look for: a baby wrapped in swaddling cloths and lying in a manger."

Tabitha suddenly said to herself, "A Saviour *has been* born? You mean Mary has *already* had her baby? And I missed it? I have to get back to Bethlehem right away and find Joseph to see if they're all right!"

She was about to fly away, but all of a sudden the sky was filled with all kinds of angels—thousands of them! They were all as beautiful as the first one, and all had joyful faces!

Then they all opened their mouths together and sang,

"Glory to God in highest heaven,
"and peace on earth to those with whom God is pleased."[21]

It was the most beautiful song she had ever heard! She wanted to listen to it all night, but as soon as they had finished singing, they all flew away up into heaven. Then she heard the shepherds talking with one another, saying that they needed to get to Bethlehem right away to see what this all meant.

Tabitha knew what she had to do, so she flew and flew as fast as she could back to the town to find them. She thought about what she had just seen. "I can hardly wait to tell Matzo about the beautiful angels. I wonder if he'll even believe me. And not just one this time, but thousands! Their voices were beautiful."

As she looked toward the town, she saw the star shining brightly in the night sky. She knew that if she followed the star she would find Mary and Joseph. Soon she saw Dan, but he was tied up outside a stable. Where were Mary and Joseph?

As Tabitha flew down, she saw Matzo sitting on Dan's back. "Matzo! Matzo!" she cried. "Wait until I tell you what I've seen! It was the most beautiful sight ever!"

"Tabitha!" said Matzo as she flew down and land on Dan's back. "I don't know where you've been, but wait till I tell you what *I've* seen!"

To be continued tomorrow...

chapter twenty-five

Jesus Is Born!

"Matzo, it was almost too much to believe!" said Tabitha. "First I saw some shepherds in a field, so I went close to them. Suddenly, an angel appeared in the sky, shining like the sun! He told the shepherds that a Saviour had been born in Bethlehem and that they needed to look for a baby in swaddling cloths lying in a manger. Then suddenly the sky was filled with thousands of angels, all singing beautiful songs of praise to God!"

Matzo had a very peaceful expression on his face. He said, "Tabitha, that sounds wonderful. I'm sure it was very beautiful."

But Tabitha could see that he was thinking about something else. She wondered what could be more important than seeing thousands of angels in the sky praising God for the Saviour's birth. Suddenly she realized what was more important: the Saviour was really born! She had been so excited by the angels that she forgot *why* they even came in the first place!

Tabitha said, "Matzo, the *Saviour* is born—Mary and Joseph's baby is born! Where is he?"

Matzo said, "I think the angels told you that already."

"The angels?" said Tabitha. "Oh, yeah; he will be 'in swaddling cloths lying in a manger.' Are those the swaddling cloths that Abby and Rachel made before we left Nazareth? Wait a second—a manger? But that's just a feeding bowl for animals. It's just a trough that horses and sheep and cows eat from!"

"That's right," said Matzo. "He's in there." Matzo pointed to the little cave right next to them.

"He's right there?" she asked. "Can we…can we go in and see him?"

"I think it would be all right," said Matzo. So he, Tabitha and Dan slowly walked toward the door of the barn. They could see light through the cracks, as if a candle or lantern was lit inside. They silently crept up to the door and tried to look in.

Tabitha could just see the side of Mary's face. She was more beautiful than ever! And Joseph's face was shining, almost like an angel! The two of them looked completely happy and completely blessed.

But of course, more than anything, the animals wanted to see the newborn baby—Jesus. Dan pushed at the door, and it opened a little. Joseph looked up and said, "Dan, Tabitha, Matzo—come on in." The three of them crept quietly toward the manger where Jesus was lying. When they got close enough to see His radiant face, they all bowed down to the ground. They didn't know exactly why, but they knew they needed to. This was not an ordinary baby; this was the Son of God.

After a minute, they looked up again. Everything was so peaceful. Then Mary began to sing. Matzo recognized it as the same song Mary sang when they were visiting Elizabeth.

"My heart rejoices in the Lord,
"My heart rejoices in my God
"He has shown His great love
"And His favour to me
"My heart rejoices in the Lord."[22]

It was beautiful. Matzo always loved to hear Mary's voice, but this time it was almost as if other voices were singing with her. Tabitha, listening carefully, said, "I recognize those voices—I just heard them a little while ago!" The three animals looked at each other in amazement. Mary was leading a choir of angels! What a glorious sound.

Soon they heard other voices and then a gentle knock. Mary looked toward the door, and her face beamed. "Elizabeth," she said, and in stepped Elizabeth with a baby in her arms, Zacharias, and Phoebe.

"We followed the star here," said Zacharias. But as soon as they looked at the baby in the manger, they too bowed their faces to the ground before the newborn King. And they could hear the music too. It was still going on even though Mary had stopped singing.

Zacharias smiled and said, "For to us a child is born, to us a son is given, and the government will be on his shoulders. And he will be called Wonderful Counselor, Mighty God, Everlasting Father, Prince of Peace."[23]

They embraced one another and exchanged greetings. Matzo was glad to see Phoebe—they had grown to be close friends while Matzo stayed with her family a few months before. He introduced her to Tabitha and Dan. It took Tabitha a while to get comfortable with a cat so close, but Matzo reassured her that Phoebe was friendly.

Soon they heard talking and whispering outside. The door cracked open a bit, and Joseph welcomed the unknown visitors. Tabitha said, "The shepherds are here!" And sure enough, a few scruffy but joyful men, along with some sheep, came into the small stable.

Matzo heard them say, "It is just as the angel said." And it happened again; as soon as they saw the baby Jesus, they bowed down to the ground and worshipped.

Soon Matzo and Tabitha made their way over to Mary and Joseph. Mary said, "Oh, Matzo, isn't this wonderful? God has sent His promised Saviour—a Saviour for the whole world! And we are part of it all!" She looked around at the unusual collection of people and animals in the small stable. "We've been through so much in the last few months since the angel first came. It hasn't always been easy, and there have been times when I didn't know how things were going to work out. But Matzo, if I've learned anything, I've learned that nothing is impossible for God!"

Matzo repeated, "Nothing is impossible for God!"

This is the end of Matzo's journey. Or perhaps I should say it's really just the beginning...

Endnotes

1   Luke 1:31–32, CEV.

2   Luke 1:35, CEV.

3   Luke 1:36, CEV.

4   Luke 1:37, CEV.

5   Luke 1:38, CEV.

6   Isaiah 7:14, NKJV.

7   Jeremiah 32:17, NKJV.

8   Matthew 1:20–21, CEV.

9   Isaiah 7:14, NKJV.

10 Luke 1:46–49, author's paraphrase.

11 Luke 1:49, author's paraphrase.

12 Luke 1:18, NIV.

13 Micah 5:2, CEV.

14 Matthew 1:21, CEV.

15 Psalm 23:1–4, ESV.

16 Psalm 23:5, ESV.

17 Psalm 23:5–6, ESV.

18 Isaiah 9:6, NIV.

19 Psalm 23:4, ESV.

20 Amos 3:7, NLT.

21 Luke 2:14, NLT.

22 Luke 1:46–49, author's paraphrase.

23 Isaiah 9:6, NIV.

Also by Kevin and Anne MacMillan

Christmas at Mole Run is a 25-chapter Advent story of the small animal community at Mole Run. Joel the mole's father disappeared two years ago, and now Joel works feverishly to rebuild the family home, destroyed by a spring flood, before Christmas. With the help of his friends Othello the owl and Pocket the ground squirrel and encouragement from the entire community, Joel prepares for the return of his mother and younger siblings. But a letter from relatives in the east causes all of Mole Run to become a hubbub of activity! And who is the mysterious stowaway on the train whose heart is set on Mole Run?

Kevin and Anne MacMillan have gratefully spent three decades in full-time local church ministry, serving in creative arts, teaching, preaching and pastoral care. They have written children's books, including *Christmas at Mole Run* and the *Matzo* trilogy, as well as several stage productions and musicals that have been produced at their church in Saskatoon, Saskatchewan, Canada. They have two married adult children and six wonderful grandchildren.